WEIRDO 9

SPOOKY WEIRD!

Scholastic Press
345 Pacific Highway Lindfield NSW 2070
An imprint of Scholastic Australia Pty Limited (ABN 11 000 614 577)
PO Box 579 Gosford NSW 2250
www.scholastic.com.au

Part of the Scholastic Group
Sydney • Auckland • New York • Toronto • London • Mexico City
• New Delhi • Hong Kong • Buenos Aires • Puerto Rico

First published by Scholastic Australia in 2017.
Text copyright © Anh Do, 2017.
Illustrations copyright © Jules Faber, 2017.

National Library of Australia Cataloguing-in-Publication entry
Creator: Do, Anh, author.
Title: Spooky weird / Anh Do; Illustrator: Jules Faber.
ISBN: 9781760276775 (paperback)
Series: Do, Anh. WeirDo; 9.
Target Audience: For primary school age.
Subjects: Halloween—Juvenile fiction.
Halloween costumes—Juvenile fiction.
Other Creators/Contributors: Faber, Jules, 1971- illustrator.

Typeset in Grenadine MVB, Push Ups and Lunch Box.

Printed in China by RR Donnelley.
Scholastic Australia's policy, in association with RR Donnelley,
is to use papers that are renewable and made efficiently
from wood grown in responsibly managed forests, so as to
minimise its environmental footprint.

15 14 13 12 11 10 9   20 21 22 23/2

ANH DO

Illustrated by JULES FABER

WEiRDO9

SPOOKY WEIRD!

A SCHOLASTIC PRESS BOOK
FROM SCHOLASTIC AUSTRALIA

I love Halloween. It's <u>so</u> **much fun** dressing up in costumes and walking around the neighborhood with **your friends**.

Henry always wears something that makes me **laugh**. Like the time he dressed up as a **tree**.

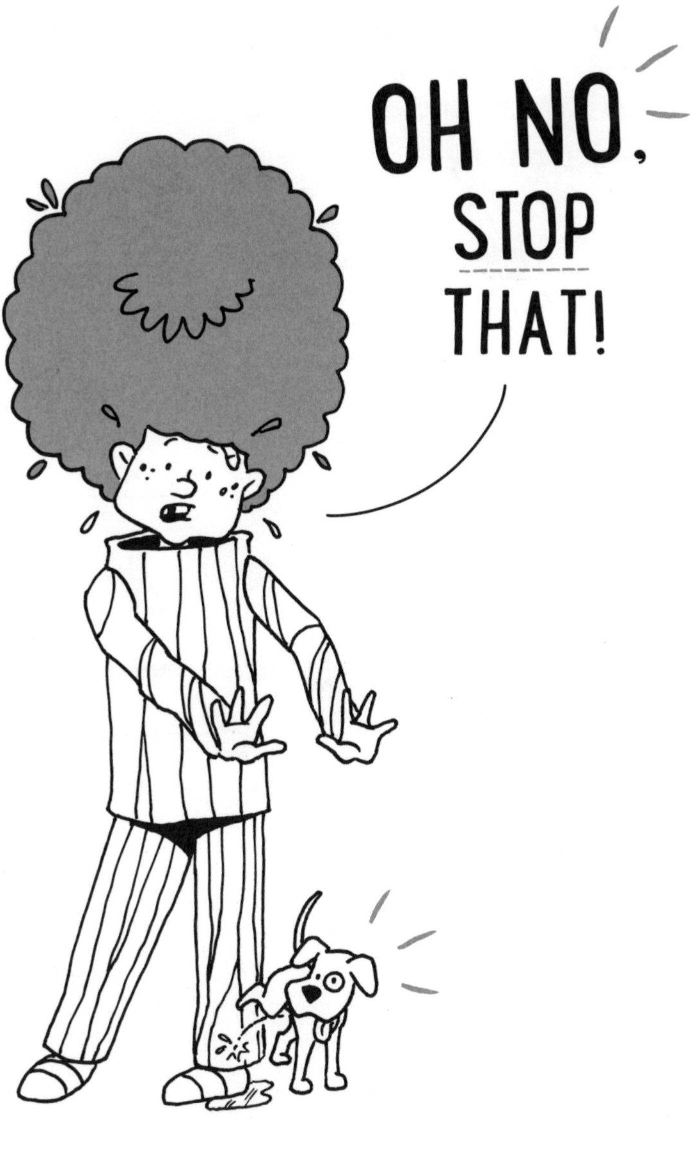
OH NO, STOP THAT!

Last year, Henry dressed up as a target.

It was **great** until we walked past some people doing **archery!**

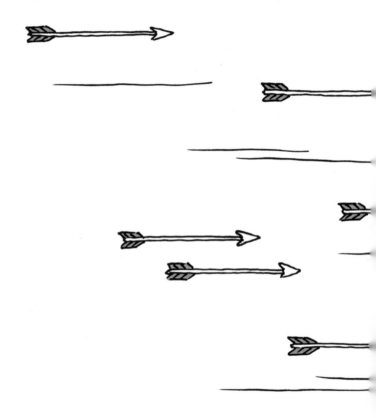

But there's **one** thing about Halloween that's even better than Henry's **funny** costumes...

It's the **one night** of the year where grown-ups hand out lollies **everywhere** you look!

WOOHOO!

Even the **dentist** gives out lollies!

BUT DON'T FORGET TO BRUSH.

I love lollies that look like **false teeth**. We all pretend to be just like Granddad!

In school, Miss Franklin was planning **trick-or-treating** for our class. First, we had to pair up for craft time—we were going to make our own Halloween <u>costumes!</u>

Miss Franklin pointed to Wendy...

YOU GO WITH HENRY, PLEASE.

'Mullet,' she said, 'you team up with Clare.
And **Bella**... You go with—'

HMM . . .

Hans Some and I were sitting up <u>REALLY</u> straight, to get noticed. We **both** wanted to be chosen to pair up with **Bella!**

'**Bella,**' Miss Franklin said, 'you go with **Weir.**'

Bella reached over and we **high-fived.**

WE ARE GOING TO MAKE THE COOLEST COSTUMES!

It was going to be **heaps of fun** making them together.

Once I made a **MUMMY** costume out of
toilet paper . . .

...but after it **rained** I looked like I'd been

FLUSHED down the toilet!

My **Bag of Chips Vending Machine**
costume was pretty cool, though!

my
vending
machine
costume

real vending machine

In fact, it was a **HUGE HIT!**

But somehow I had to TOP that and come up with something

completely new

and

completely

AWESOME!

CHAPTER 2

After school, Bella and I were walking home to my place. We were going to get started on our Halloween costumes!

'What about a pair of zombies?' said Bella. 'Or mad scientists?'

'Or an astronaut?' I suggested.

WITH A
ROCKET?!
THAT
COULD BE
COOL!

WHY DID THE
ASTRONAUTS TRIP
TO MARS
GO WRONG?

HE DIDN'T
PLANET
PROPERLY!

'Hey, look,' said Bella, pointing to a **sign** on a telegraph pole.

'I hope they find her,' said Bella.

'Me too,' I agreed. 'Poor Molly.'

As we neared my house, we saw **Blockhead** and **FiDo** at the front door.

'What if we **dressed up** as Blockhead and FiDo?' I said to Bella.

WOOF! WOOF!

'That would be **so funny!**' said Bella, laughing. 'But they'd be **pretty hard** costumes to make!'

Bella was right. Those ideas wouldn't be **easy!**

Plus we had to find materials. The first thing we had to do was see what kind of **stuff** we could find in the **garage**.

We said **hello** to Blockhead and FiDo, but they barely gave us a **woof**. In fact, they both looked **really sad.**

WHAT'S UP WITH THEM?

Inside the house,

it didn't get

any

better!

so sad!

super sad!

'What's going on?' I asked.

WHY DO YOU ALL LOOK SO SAD?

No-one said anything right away...
but then Sally spoke up.

What was Sally talking about?!

She looked like she might **cry!**

'We're **moving away**!' said Sally with a sniffle.

SNIFF!

Mum and Dad sat me down and told me that Sally was right. That we – **the Do family** – were moving away!

I couldn't **believe** it!

But why?

Mum and Dad explained that we needed to
move out of our house and **find another
one** ... but the problem was, they couldn't find
anything nearby that they could afford.

So they had no choice but to move us to a **new place** that was really **FAR away!**

We had to **change schools** and everything!

'But I don't want to leave,' I said. 'I **love** our house, our street, my school ...'

And then I looked at 𝓑𝓮𝓵𝓵𝓪.

'And my **FRIENDS!**'

'I don't want to live **anywhere** but here!' I said.

Anywhere else would feel like another **planet**!

'When?' I asked. 'When do we have to move?'

'I'm sorry, Weir,' said Mum, 'but we have to pack up and leave next week.'

NEXT WEEK?

This was the worst news ever.

CHAPTER 3

We couldn't find **anything** in the garage that we could use to make our Halloween costumes.

Bella was searching **everywhere** ... but I was too busy thinking about how I'd be moving away so soon ...

It would be my <u>last</u> Halloween with my friends!

A cloud of dust rose as Bella picked up two towels and **shook** them.

COUGH!

COUGH!

Once the dust settled, Bella said,

'Superhero capes?'

SHOWER LADY AND BATH MAN TO THE RESCUE!

'Whenever there are **wet** people who need **drying**—we'll be there!' I said.

'Hmm, maybe not,' said Bella.

'What about these?' said Bella, picking up a few pairs of Mum's <u>old stockings</u>.

OCTOPUS LEGS?

We'd need WAY more legs than that!

'There's nothing useful here,' I said. 'Maybe I shouldn't bother going trick-or-treating...'

Bella looked a bit disappointed, but then she **spotted** something in the corner.

'We just have to look **harder!**' she said. 'We can turn **anything** into a costume!'

SEE THIS
WASHING
BASKET?

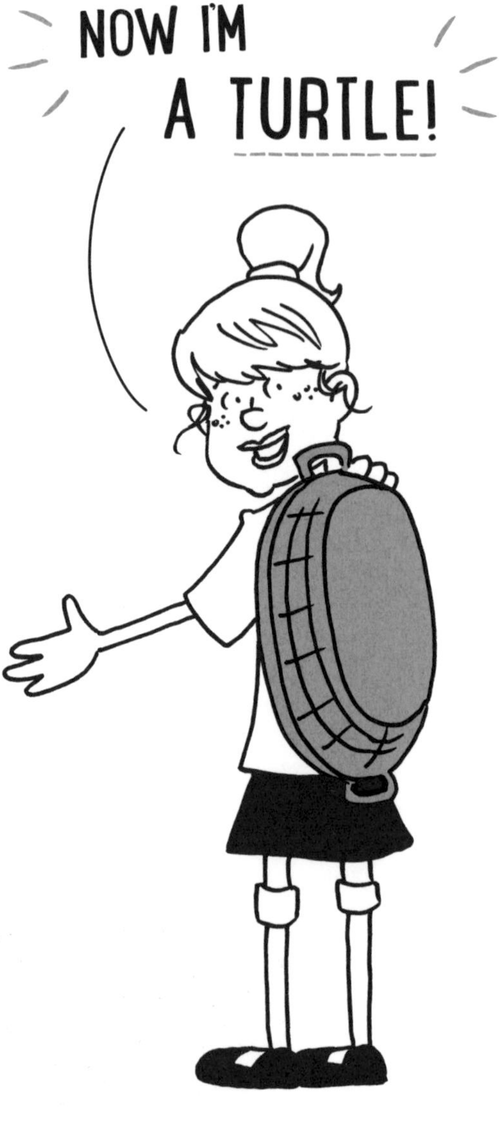
NOW I'M
A TURTLE!

Bella pulled out one of Sally's old **hula hoops.**

UMM . . .
WHAT COULD WE DO
WITH A HULA HOOP?

Next, Bella began wriggling into Granddad's **sleeping bag**.

She was thinking hard. What was she going to come up with next? **A burrito?**

UMM . . .

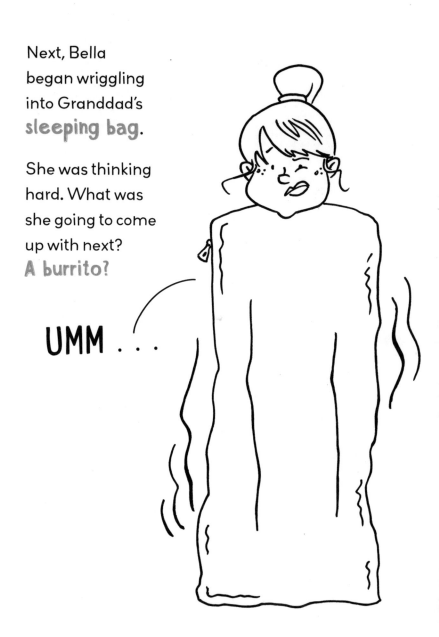

I'M AN . . . UMM . . . I'M A <u>SLEEPING</u> <u>BAG!</u>

A **sleeping bag?!**

Bella's ideas were <u>TERRIBLE!</u>

But they were also **pretty funny!**

HAHA HAHA!

Bella laughed too and started **wobbling**!

'Uh-oh, I think I'm stuck!' she said, losing her balance.

WHOAAAAA!

Bella **tipped** over and **bumped** a shelf by the wall. At that moment, something from way up top **fell right**

on my

head.

BUMP!

SLAP!

'What's that?' asked Bella, getting up and looking a bit **dizzy!**

I brushed the dust off the bag that had fallen on **me**.

'They're just a big old bag of **green balloons** ...' I said, tossing them aside.

NOTHING USEFUL . . .

Our garage search had given us NOTHING to use for our Halloween costumes! We needed to come up with **another plan**.

'Hi guys!' said Dad, popping his head in the garage.

He was carrying a **big bowl** of grapes. **Green** and **round** and **juicy**. 'Want a snack?'

TRUST ME, THEY TASTE GRAPE!

'Thanks, Dad,' I said, as Bella and I
helped ourselves to a bunch each.

MMM.

YUM.

They were **delicious.**

And then suddenly it **hit us!**

'We can use the **BALLOONS** to make us look like bunches of **GRAPES!**' I said, high-fiving Bella.

WHAT A
GRAPE IDEA!

CHAPTER 4

It can be pretty fun when you get to take a day off school ... But **NOT** when your granddad's taking you to SEE YOUR NEW SCHOOL!
The one that's far, far away!

COME ON, WEIR,
YOU'LL MAKE **NEW**
FRIENDS IN NO TIME.

Granddad left me at **my new class**, then went away to take Sally to hers.

My new teacher's name was **Mr Lean**.

He had these **big furry** eyebrows that made him look **REALLY** cranky!

very cranky eyebrows!

More like **Mr Mean!**

Anyone could look mean with those!

mean!

mean!

mean!

DID YOU DO
YOUR HOMEWORK?!

NO! MY
EYEBROWS
ATE IT!

Mr Mean – I mean, Mr Lean – looked at me.

'And what's your name?' he asked.

I was about to tell him the truth about my name, but I didn't want him to laugh at me. So I made something up.

I'M . . . UM . . . HANS . . . SOME.

There! That was better than admitting my name was WEIRDO!

But **guess what** the teacher did next?

HA HA HA HA-HA! HANS SOME!

He rolled around the floor LAUGHING!

'What's your brother's name?' he said.
'Fear Some!? Or your mum –
Awe Some?!'

'And what about your dad?' said Mr Mean.

By now, the **whole class** was laughing.

BA-HA HA HA
HA HA HA!

If they all thought **HANS SOME** was a funny
name ... what were they going to think of
WEIR DO?!

Finally, Mr Lean stopped laughing and
introduced me to the class.

There was ...

Jake Green

Penny

Charles Nott

Blair   Coby Hogan   Benny

and Stella Allen

Plus there was a kid who looked
just like the REAL Hans Some...
His name was

Goode Looking!

HANS SOME?
COOL NAME.

TOTALLY
COOL.

I was **so busy** trying to look cool, like the **real** Hans Some, I forgot I was wearing

my dad's

old shoes . . .

and

tripped._

I'd done it **again**!

This new school **WAS NOT** off to a great start!

CHAPTER 5

'I don't think *that* school is right for me,' I told Mum and Dad later that night.

'It was **really weird**.'

WEIRD?
WELL YOU'LL FIT
RIGHT IN!

Mum kept telling me it would get better. And that I'd settle in REALLY QUICKLY and make new friends in NO TIME.

But I didn't want to settle in.

I didn't want to make new friends.

I just wanted to keep the friends I already had!

Even Blockhead and FiDo were sad about the move.

STAY! STAY!

WOOF!

They **loved exploring** our street, and playing **games** in our house. But just like us, they had boxes that needed to be packed.

I had just **one day** left at **MY** school ... then it was Halloween ... and then we'd be packing up our place and leaving **for good**.

My last day at school wasn't easy. I would miss this place so much!

I'd miss Toby always **dropping things**...

OOPS!

WHOA!

I'd miss Henry **making me laugh**...

I'd even miss those birds in the playground that were always **pooping on my head!**

I was feeling **pretty sad** as I walked into my classroom after lunch. The day had gone **so fast!** I only had a couple of hours to go ...

The classroom was **empty.**

WHERE IS EVERYONE?

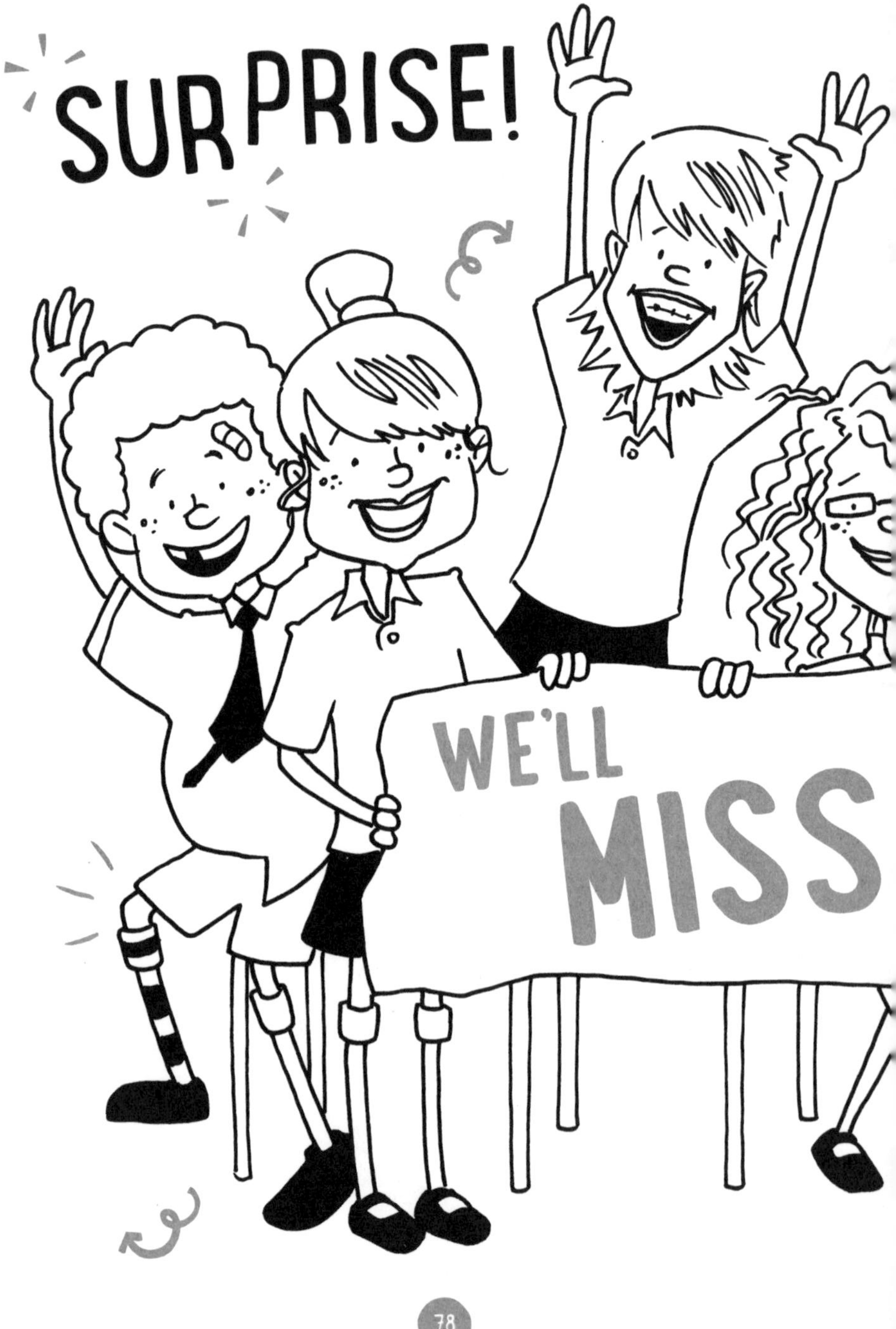
SURPRISE!
WE'LL
MISS

It turns out Bella had organised a **huge goodbye party** for me!

Miss Franklin had even made a cake that looked just like <u>me</u>!

cake me!

I slowly made my way around class, saying **goodbye** to everyone.

Even **Blake Green** was nice to me.

I'LL MISS YOU, YOU BIG WEIRDO. *SNIFF!*

Saying goodbye to Henry and Bella was going to be **the hardest**. Luckily I was going to see them again later for **Trick-or-Treating**.

We **promised** we'd **write** to each other all the time! And **visit** as much as possible!

Henry even sang me a <u>farewell poem</u>.

THERE ONCE WAS A BOY CALLED WEIRDO.
YES, HIS NAME WAS WEIR,
♪ OH!
HE MAKES US
LAUGH,
HE'S A CLOWN-
AND-A-HALF,

THAT'S WHY HE'S MY FRIEND AND MY HERO!

On our way to my house, to finish off our GRAPE costumes, Bella and I stopped by the place __next__ to hers.

There was a **FOR RENT** sign in the yard,
almost covered by bushes and weeds.

'Oh, that place is **super SPOOKY**,' said Bella.
'No-one wants to move in there ...'

'But why?' I asked.

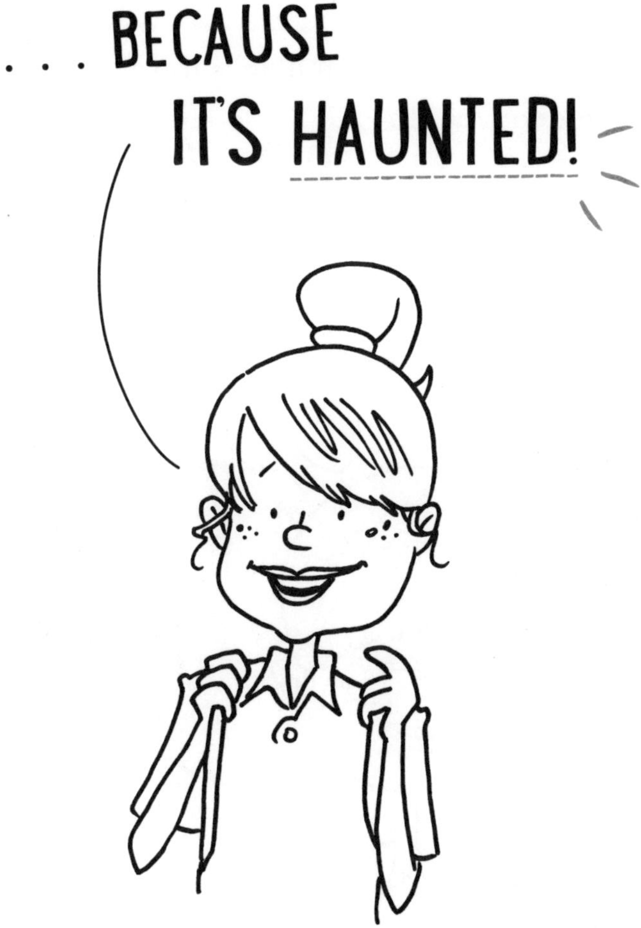
. . . BECAUSE IT'S HAUNTED!

'Come on, Bella, you don't believe that stuff, do you?' I asked.

She didn't answer, but gave me a look that said maybe she DID believe it.

HMM.

Bella told me there were **strange noises** coming out of the house ... and that no-one lived in there, but lately people swore they could hear **voices** coming from inside.

THEY CAN HEAR VOICES?

'I think people must be **imagining** things,'
I said, trying to sound confident.

Just then, we heard a REALLY SPOOOOOOKY
voice call out from inside.

GO AWAY!

DO NOT
ENTER!

WOOOOO!

'Did you just hear that?' said Bella, looking panicked.

Before I could answer, we heard the voice again!

'GO AWAY!' it hissed. 'WOOOOO!'

It didn't need to tell us twice! We bolted!

AHHHH!

AHHHHH

'That place **really is** haunted,' I said.

'Told you so!' said Bella.

We were both **so relieved** to be at my house and away from that <u>creepy place</u>!

Besides, we had work to do. We had <u>hundreds</u> of **balloons** to blow up for our **grape costumes!**

There were just **SO MANY** balloons!

It was taking us forever!

But finally, Bella blew up the **very** last balloon.

With Mum's help, we attached the balloons to our clothes. Lastly, she put **two old green hats** on our heads, which looked like **leaves**!

We were ready to **TRICK OR TREAT!**

CHAPTER 7

Henry and Wendy were waiting outside to meet us.

HAPPY HALLOWEEN!

'You make a great **witch**, Wendy!' said Bella.

'Yeah, and that's a cool **ghost** costume,' I said to Henry.

GHOST? I'M NOT A GHOST.

THEN WHAT ARE YOU?

I was going to miss Henry's jokes!

Henry and Wendy loved our **grape** costumes.
I reached out to shake Henry's hand.

'Don't forget to knock on **our** door!' Mum called out. We turned and wandered back up the path to her.

We all **sang** out...

Mum and Dad dropped something **BIG** into our bags!

We were going to have a **HUGE** night, if this was how much we were going to get from every house!

We reached into our bags to find out what we'd been given.

I fished out something long. Maybe a chocolate bar?!

But it **wasn't** a chocolate bar.

A TOOTHBRUSH?!
BUT I CAN'T EAT THAT!

And Henry fished out something else.

AND TOOTHPASTE!

'Thanks Mr and Mrs Do,' said Bella, politely.

THOSE TEETH ARE GOING TO NEED A GOOD BRUSH AFTER TONIGHT!

Just as we were about to head off in search of REAL LOLLIES, Blockhead flew out of the house to join us!

ARRRR-MATEY!

'I couldn't help it,' said Mum. 'I made him a **little costume** too!'

I GUESS YOU'RE COMING WITH US!

I looked at my friends. 'Let's go!'

We had one of the **greatest nights** together.

We

talked and

laughed ...

... we ran into **other people**

from school . . .

Like Mullet . . .

DOES SOMETHING SMELL FISHY?

dressed as a mullet!

And James Nott...

dressed as a **runny nose**!

We saw some **really WEIRD** costumes too...

Like Harry
Highpants

an evil
pumpkin

and a girl
wearing a
whole bunch
of undies!

...and we collected lollies!

Loads of LOLLIES!

This was our **biggest haul EVER!**

After we were done for the night, we said our **goodbyes**. Henry and Wendy went one way and Bella and I went another. I was going to walk her home.

'Thanks for a **grape** night, you guys,' Henry called out. 'Don't stay out too long or you'll turn into **sultanas**!'

sultanas!

The house next to Bella's was even **spookier**– looking tonight.

really spooky house

Bella and I **jumped** as we heard a tiny murmur, coming from inside.

'It was nothing,' said Bella. 'Don't worry.'

But then we heard it **again!**

'Go away!' a spooky voice hissed. **'Go away!'**

YOU HEARD THAT,
RIGHT?!

Blockhead suddenly squawked and flapped and flew off! He was heading right for the house!

'Blockhead, no!' I shouted. 'Come back!'

But it was too late! He'd flown through an open window, right into the HAUNTED HOUSE!

'What do we do now?' I asked Bella.

'We go in after him, I guess …' she said, walking towards the gate.

Man, she was brave!

WAY

braver

than me!

I was so scared, all my balloons were **shaking!**

EEEEEEEEK!

We opened the gate and walked inside. We slowly tiptoed up the path, past the long grass, overgrown weeds, and the old **FOR RENT** sign.

A **spider** suddenly dropped down in front of me and I **jumped** backwards.

I **tripped** over a rock

and

fell

over.

But because I was completely covered in balloons,

I hit

the

ground . . .

and **bounced right back!**

Airbags!

That was handy!

When we finally reached the door, I lifted my hand and knocked.

KNOCK,

KNOCK,

KNOCK.

I hoped whoever, or whatever, was in there liked grapes ...

When nobody answered, I turned to go ... but I knew we couldn't leave Blockhead behind!

Just then, we heard Blockhead cry out from inside. He was calling to me!

WEIRDO!
WEIRDO!

Slowly, and bravely, I pushed the door open. It **creaked** really loudly, but not as loudly as the thumping of my heart!

THUMP!

THUMP!

THUMP!

I was **terrified**, but we had to **rescue Blockhead!**

We ducked under huge cobwebs and walked inside.

In the light of the moon, we saw Blockhead sitting on a couch next to <u>another parrot!</u>

GO AWAY!

GO AWAY!

SQUAWK!

DO NOT ENTER!

The creepy voice we'd heard earlier belonged to the **PARROT!** A talking parrot with a broken wing!

The parrot was telling us to **go away**, but she looked perfectly happy to see us!

At the same time, me and Bella remembered something!

THE <u>MISSING</u> BIRD SIGN!

'**Molly?** Is that you?' we asked.

ME MOLLY!
GO AWAY!
ME MOLLY!

CHAPTER 8

We carried Blockhead and Molly next door to Bella's house, then we **found** the phone number on the **missing poster** and called **Molly's owner**.

MISSING!

She was **so relieved** to hear that we'd found her bird!

She turned up at Bella's house within **minutes!**

The lady and Molly even **looked alike!**

GO AWAY!
I'VE
MISSED
YOU!
GO AWAY!

'Hello, **my little Molly!**' said the lady.

'You see,' she explained. 'I live in a house with a yard that was too small for a **guard dog**. So I got a **guard parrot** instead! I trained Molly to say things like **GO AWAY** and **DO NOT ENTER!**'

OH, THAT'S WHY SHE SAYS THOSE THINGS!

'She's a **perfectly lovely** bird,' said the lady, giving **Molly** a cuddle. 'She actually loves company.'

It felt **so good** to help Molly find her way back home ... and it was **awesome** to have solved the mystery of the **spooky voice** in the **haunted house** ...

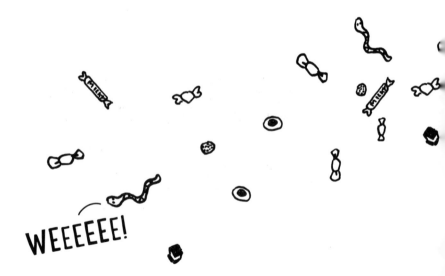

WEEEEEE!

...a house that wasn't so **HAUNTED** after all...

I **ran home** to tell

Mum and Dad

all about it.

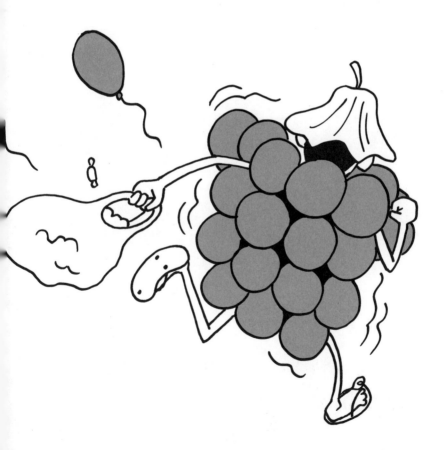

CHAPTER 9

Mum and Dad went to look at the <u>NOT</u> HAUNTED house the very next day. After a few **quick calls** and a few **big talks** …

… we decided to **RENT IT!**

We didn't have to move away, after all! We only needed to move **down the street!**

And **best of all** ... we didn't have to **change schools**!

We all love our **new house**. It's a bit **rundown** in places ...

LOOK,
ANOTHER WINDOW!

...and you can get **lost** in the <u>wild</u> **yard**...

HELP!
WHERE AM I?
WHICH WAY TO
THE HOUSE?

But there's nothing we can't work around!

And one of the **coolest** things?

The house even has an attic!

COME ON,
LET'S CHECK IT OUT!

I thought we were going to find **spiderwebs** and **dark, spooky corners**…

but you **won't** believe it…

The attic

was

filled

with . . .

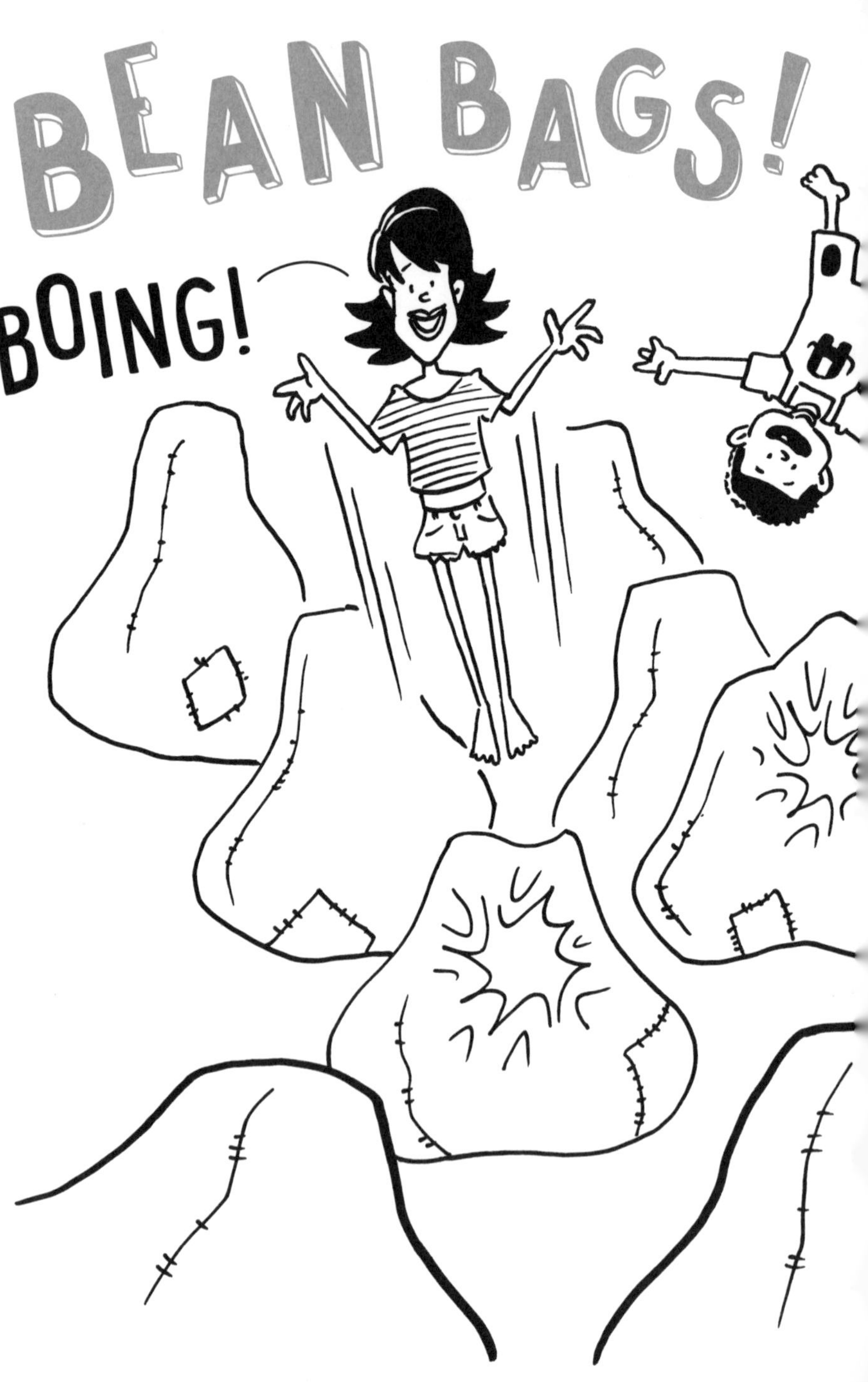
BEAN BAGS!
BOING!

Blockhead has a **new friend**, who comes over to visit in the afternoons, now that her wing has healed.

And it turns out her owner – **Miss Lovely** – lives just behind us! She and Granddad **love chatting** over the fence! She thinks he's really funny.

It's awesome that Blockhead and Granddad have made new friends.

But I think I'm the luckiest one of all.

My new neighbour is just the

BEST!

For Nicole—

the **best** designer!

FROM ANH

ACKNOWLEDGEMENTS

FROM JULES

For everyone who **loves** to draw. Don't **ever** stop.

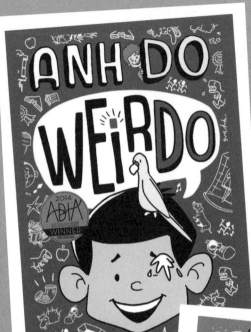

Book 1

GOT IT!

bird

Book 2

GOT IT!

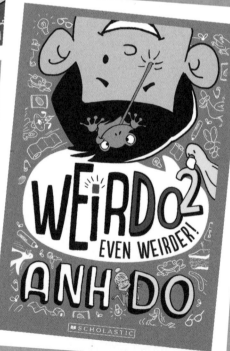

ladybug!

COLLECT
THEM ALL!

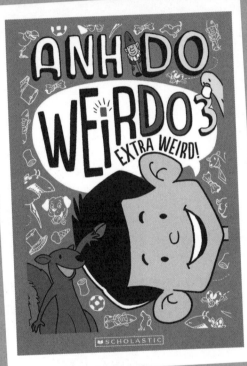

Book 3

GOT IT!

gnomes

flying soccer ball

COLLECT THEM ALL!

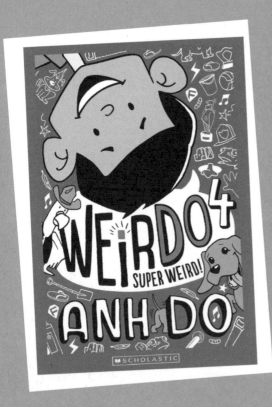

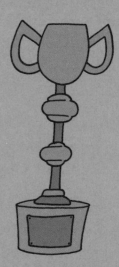

trophy ↗

← Book 4

GOT IT!

pet rock ↘

pineapple ↙

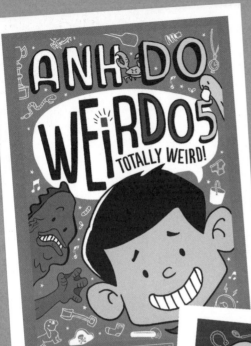

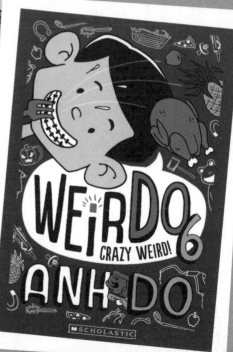

Book 5

Book 6

Book 7

GOT IT!

Book 8

GOT IT!

COLLECT THEM ALL!

YOU CAN NEVER HAVE TOO MANY WEIRDOS

Book 9

GOT IT!

pie

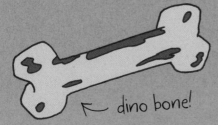

dino bone!

Roger